The Bog Hag

Jacquelynn Lyon

ISBN: 9798555531124
Imprint: Independently published

Cover design by: Meridith Richter
Library of Congress Control Number: 2018675309
Printed in the United States of America

The Bog Hag

By Jacquelynn Lyon

I was a little over four hundred years when she arrived. Young for the ages, but old for what I used to be.

I felt the vibrations before I saw her: dainty feet, an uneven tilt to her steps, sloppy, like pancakes hitting a hot skillet and splattering. I bet my last five teeth that she was a late walker, late to crawl, late to lumber across my path. I curled my lips back and grinned wildly, of course, something like her gait wouldn't matter much after this.

She took a couple steps across the wooden planks, barefoot — like she was tempting me without a prayer to her name—and then stopped. I waited for another minute for those prime, pale ankles to come within my reach, but she just stood there.

I peeked quietly out of my hole and scowled; a head was hanging down over the edge of the railing. Rivers of lank, blond hair cascaded toward the water accompanied by a small face, frowning mouth, cherry nose, and sharp eyes.

Her eyes were pale green and sat under large, expressive eyebrows, thick and rounded things— like fat caterpillars.

Her mouth quirked to the side and her small features bunched up. I snorted loudly. She was wickedly beautiful; I would've eaten her right then and there if she wasn't looking at me with the type of directness only arrogance can summon.

I presented my darkened teeth to her, spreading my long, thin fingers out and leaning into the dim light as the muddy water parted around me.

"Well, well, well," I said as I flexed my fingers and coated my words with syrupy sweetness, "they really do serve themselves up on a platter these days."

I licked my lips rapaciously.

The young woman tilted her head to the side, and her golden rivers of hair rippled in place. She observed me from upside down. "I don't think so," she finally spoke and then flashed me her fine fingers, chubby and small to match her figure. One golden rose ring shone from her pointer finger, and I hissed.

"Royal brat."

She shrugged and finally stood up properly to peer down at me. "Come out," she said.

I scowled. "You may have immunity, but I don't take orders. You are all temporary." I squatted down in the sludge and grumbled. "I am the trees and wind, the dark of the waters. You will pass. I will not."

"Yeah, yeah." She flicked her wrist. "I just wanna see."

My eyes turned to slits. "What the inside of my belly looks like? I'd be happy to accommodate."

She could have only been around eighteen, young, blithe, angry about something I couldn't guess at.

She cushioned her chin on her folded arms and blinked down. "I wish I looked like you."

I made a face, more of one than usual. "The little girl wants the devil under her skin. How special."

The girl rolled her eyes in a magnificent circle. "I'm not little," she said loudly, "and you know what I mean."

I was overtaken with a strange puzzlement with the girl. "What's your name, little bird?"

She growled. "Not. Little," she repeated. "I'm almost twenty and I'm not dumb enough to give my name to a witch."

I shrugged. "It seemed like you were."

"Ugh." She leaned over the railing. "I wish all I had to do was sit under a bridge and tease strangers. And my mom says *I'm* the ungrateful one."

"Tease and then eat them," I said in an exasperated tone. "You're leaving out the most important part."

She hummed lowly. "What do people taste like?"

I smacked my lips together. "Like juicy, juicy pig meat, but more tender."

She laughed with a rich, full sound. "Liar."

I frowned at her. "Don't you have places to be? You are a royal."

She scrunched her face up and pushed her loose blond hair back. "Why do you think I'm here? I'm trying *not* to have things to do."

I looked her up and down. "I don't remember being invited to the birth of such a brat." I commented dryly. "Is that Hessia family spurning me again?"

She sighed loudly. "Nah." The girl reached into her pocket and flashed another ring in my direction; this one was an ornate blue sparrow. "I'm not from here."

"Ah." I mulled that over for a second. "It's a good thing they already extended their immunity to you. Just remember to invite me to the wedding or I'll—"

"Or you'll unleash the gale-force winds and raise the water and curse our children. I've heard."

I grimaced and peeled my lips back from my teeth. "Do they not have manners where you're from?" I asked mildly. "Or are you simply in the mood to push your luck?"

I wandered farther out of my tunnel. The pale sunlight bathed my earthy hair, covered in twigs and dirt and the wiggling life. One bird pecked away for earthworms there. The girl stiffened as she examined me, taking in my puffy, green skin, wrecked knuckles, parched mouth, the hunch of my back, and long, mud-caked gown. I smiled so widely I think I almost cracked my face in half.

She placed her chin on her arms again. "I'm not here to have manners," she said lowly. "You don't have any, as I can tell. Why should I?" She sighed. "What's this bargain with the devil again?"

I shook my head. "Too high a price," I muttered quietly and tilted my chin upward, eyes glowing ember yellow and long nose catching the light. I was now fully exposed in the swampy waters. "Are you sure you still want to look like me, lovely bird?"

She raised her eyebrows. "Oh yes," she said simply. "Who wouldn't?" She smiled an uncomplicated smile and then turned around. "Prince Jace will probably send out the dogs if I am gone any longer, but," she pushed her hair aside and looked over her shoulder, "I'm Tuck."

"Tuck," I rolled the name around on my tongue and tried to consume the vowels and suck the marrow out of the consonants. My expression soured.

"Not my real name, obviously," she said with a smirk, "but everyone calls me that. Or used to."

I was still gnashing on something I couldn't quite chew. "Fascinating." I said dryly and swept into a mock bow. "Lady Tuck then."

She waved. "They told me there was a powerful Bog Hag in these parts." She examined me. "It was nice to meet you."

Now she has manners, I noted bitterly.

The strange girl turned around and started walking. I grinned after her and imagined sinking my teeth around her pale throat, letting the red droplets spill out and color my muddy brown waters. I blinked a couple times and then grumbled about the royals— they could always do more to me, it seemed, including being nuisances.

Tuck's unsteady footsteps disappeared without a trace, and I closed my eyes and sank into the warm, earthy waters again.

I was around four hundred at the time . . . young for the steady trees and arching rivers, old for what I used to be.

"On a scale of one to ten, how clever do you actually find fairies?"

Tuck was sitting at the edge of the water, pale blue skirts crumpled under her and feet narrowly close to the lapping pond.

I sighed loudly in exasperation. "Go home, little birdie." I waved my hand in the air. "Your presence isn't requested here."

She glanced up mildly. "That isn't even a proper answer. Are Centaurs truly as health obsessed as they say? My uncle met one, and he said all the poor fellow could talk about was his kneecaps and the next plague. A right hypochondriac."

My left eyebrow twitched. "Why don't you go ask one?"

Tuck reclined backward into the dappled sunlight. "Does it look like I know many Mythics? I'm asking *you*," she said loudly,

I glowered over at her. "You must have books." I said with a sneer. "Rooms full of them I hear, houses full."

Tuck crossed her arms over her chest. "And what would the court say? That's what Matilda would remind me. The future queen burying herself in otherworldly material." Tuck snorted noisily. "I would never get away with it."

"But you get away with conversing with a Bog Hag?" I reminded her pointedly, mostly so I could return to my hunting. "How progressive."

She cracked an almost-smile. "Oh, yes, they call it a glorious new diplomatic mission." She lifted her chin up proudly. "One only for the foreign queen of course. Taking up friendship with the local terrors."

I scoffed. "I take it they think you're out riding?"

She didn't look back at me. "They think I'm out weeping." She took a deep breath and glanced at me. "A Kiliok tradition before a wedding.”

“Kiliok.” I rolled that word around in my mouth. “A northern queen, very well.”

She didn’t so much as nod as keep staring. “Do you know of us?”

I shrugged loosely, destabilizing clumps of dirt that rolled down my shoulder-tops. “I know of many things.”

A faint smile ghosted over her lips again. “Cool.”

I shook my head and returned to examining over the warm waters. “You know, perhaps you are safe from me eating you, but there are other scarier things in this forest.” I hit her with a hard look. “It’s old. And the earth here is not as kind as me.”

She looked nonplussed. “Scarier than you?” She grinned boldly. “I highly doubt it.”

I huffed. “Perhaps you should act like it,” I groused plainly, “and leave. That’s what you do when you’re scared if you’d like to know.”

“So touchy!” Tuck crowed. “It almost sounds like you like to be alone.” She said cheekily, and I searched the waters for the nearest large fish.

“How did you guess?” I retorted in a flat tone, and she laughed.

“Go on,” she said cheerily. “Catch something.”

My lips curled back again. “You’re already here.”

“Oh, come now, we already had this out.” She gathered her

legs to her chest, reminding me of a small child or a cat. "I want to be you and you want to eat me, neither of us can have what we want."

I gave her one last placid look before plunging my hand into the water; my long nails pierced the fish before it could even twitch. It was large, the largest one I had had in months, and I smiled greedily.

I wrenched the catfish from the waters and held its flopping body in my hands. "Watch carefully, young queen." My eyes gleamed. "You may learn something."

I sank my teeth into its moist flesh and waited for it to stop squirming before tearing at its soft meat.

"Cool," was the last word I heard before I dug in. I would have rolled my eyes all over again if I wasn't preoccupied.

Tuck was still there when I finished and asked me how I found Rocs— were they slightly above dog intelligence, or was it true you could hold a conversation with one? I tried to fade back into the muddy waters, but we ended up bickering about enchanted animals and where to best summon storms from.

∞ ∞ ∞

"I don't suppose you ever leave this place."

I came to expect Tuck's weekly visits, two full moons' worth so far. I didn't turn around this time as she approached.

"Not like you do, princess," I said somberly as I oozed my way toward the midday sun; she always came around midday.

"Ha, right," she said lightly and took her usual seat by my waters. "You could go wherever you please though."

I raised my eyebrows and a stick dislodged from my hair and bumped my cheek before making a small *plop* into the water. I traced patterns in the algae in front of me. "And where would I go?"

Tuck made a soft sound. "I dunno. Another swamp? The coasts? The artic wilds? You must have hobbies."

I fixed her with an even look. "Between you and the errant fisherman, I'm afraid I have no time for hobbies," I said gingerly and she let out her little snorting laugh.

"I'm serious."

I tsked. "I'm as bound to this swamp as you are bound to the land instead of sky. It is how it is," I said slowly.

She just nodded a little sardonically. "Finally, straight answers."

I sighed. "Have you come to quiz me again about Dwarven bathing habits?"

She smiled brightly. "That and, unfortunately, it seems Jace will have me do all the work for him."

"The Hessians usually do." I peered down at my long nails. "What is it?"

Her large green eyes held me for a second. "Are you free next Friday?"

I chuckled lowly. "Let me check my schedule."

Tuck returned the wicked smile. "I was told it was best to invite the local powerful Mythics." She winked. "Wouldn't want to snub anyone."

"After all the other visits? I wouldn't mind being snubbed at this point." I grumbled.

"Come now," she said heartily. "Scare a few nobles, get a free meal, remind the world that's it's mortal and weak and easily eaten by strange green ladies. You must like being invited to these sorts of things for a reason."

"It's a matter of honor," I said tightly, "respect."

She examined me again. "I see."

"No, you don't." I snapped back and she laughed once more.

"Always so prickly!" she tutted. "You're lucky I like you, or I wouldn't not invite you to my wedding."

"You just like oddities," I said in a dismissive tone. "Bored nobles like yourself so easily lose their common sense." I eyed her. "But I'll come. I do like to see the children's faces when I arrive." I finished with a sharp grin.

"That's the spirit," she beamed. "Now," she settled down, "do you think the Gods of night are better lovers than those of the sun? I've heard rumors going both ways."

"Of course, the moon ones are better," I said as I settled down deep into the silt of the pond bed with only my head exposed. "The Sun God's are more self-centered than a Nymph discovering her own reflection . . ."

I wished so desperately for Tuck to leave, but I never was good at giving into myself either.

∞∞∞

The day came, a breezy morning in spring when the sun erupted out from between the clouds and flowers set to bloom. There were very few flowers by my bridge, but I sensed them opening elsewhere. Their scent thick in the air, rejoicing in the soil, and covered in red lady bugs and fat yellow bees that feared the dark of my woods.

I dragged myself up and quickly feasted, spending two days gorging and fueling myself for the journey. I cast golden protective circles around my limbs and throat. I caked more mud into my hair and fashioned branches into crooked wings off my hunched shoulders.

A Bog Hag had to play her part after all; I had to show them what eternity looked like.

The actual exit from my realm was long and unnerving, the familiar suck of my life force and the shuddering of every nerve in my body was taxing. I hefted myself slowly out of the water, groaning slightly like an oak tree against a typhoon.

The last push was always the hardest.

Solid ground was a cold kick to the teeth, and I was very glad no one wandered near the edges of my bog as I finished the exodus. I took several deep, wincing breaths and straightened myself out.

"All right," I said calmly, "yes."

I summoned my strength back to me, and the color returned to my cheeks and my hands steadied; it would be easy after that.

I did not walk the city streets, as that would in many ways ruin the effect. Instead, I arrived at the palace gates as a shadow and summoned the northern winds to blow open the doors. The first set of courtiers jumped at the banging of the wood and whoosh of the breeze. I spread my arms out wide and raised myself up tall. "Good morning."

I took in the children's faces first. Oh yes— their little, bewildered stares were the cream for the cat's tongue. Their mouths were agape and eyes as wide as moons. I could only grin at the hisses and hushed whispers of the adults as they witnessed me. I strode forward and watched their chests seize up and noses turn toward the ceiling. I walked on.

The floors were covered in blood-red carpet sheathed in gold trim, and silken tapestries hung on the walls of past wars and dead heroes. I didn't bother to soften my steps or hold my dirt clumps to me. I let the soil roll to the castle floors and earthworms wiggle in my wake as they fell.

I made a beeline for the throne room and found a tall, graying man with steel eyes and a square jaw outside of it, waiting. He wore a white military uniform with a purple cape draped across his shoulders, and a golden crown glinted on his brow. I lifted my chin up.

"Kind as ever to invite me, King Gregory," I said huskily as I reached the enormous doors. I didn't have to look up to know I had the king's attention.

Every muscle in his body tightened. "It is an honor to host you, Miss Lamn." Lamn was the name of the bog I inhabited. They didn't know my real name, but that was how it was supposed to be.

I lifted my sharp chin up. "A witch always remembers loyalties, sire. We both give and take." I emphasized the "give *and* take," reminding him of the long agreement between us: the diplomacy of the sword and bread. They offered me the bread, and so I wouldn't brandish my sword. I nodded at their wisdom and exchanged a tablet of blood with the king— I would never harm his bloodline as long as he honored me.

"If you'll excuse me, Miss Lamn." He left as soon as the trade was over, and I turned back to the great hall. The crowd parted for me with enough room for a parade of horses between us. I grinned. *Oh yes, this part I like.*

I showed a nearby girl all five of my bare, busted teeth, and she made a small whimpering sound before hiding in her mother's skirts. I cackled and turn back to the main room, where the king was whispering to an advisor but making no move to approach me again. A smart man.

The Queen of the Fairies arrived shortly after and was greeted in a similar fashion. Hessia was a large kingdom and had quite a few powerful Mythics who could attend if they wanted to, but only a few would. Even I would admit that in other cases, I might have forgone the trip, but I was still a little perplexed by the future queen. I had been meeting her weekly, after all.

The locals watched me closely as I passed easily through the church doors with not so much as a twitch. *Like the devil works that simply, little fools.*

They scattered once I entered and looked in their direction.

I was unsurprised to read a different name on the parchment hanging inside the church. I shook my head at the welcoming sign: "The Wedding of Prince Jace to his betrothed Princess Nadina." I didn't know what to make of "Nadina," but perhaps everyone comes up with names for ourselves that are wildly different than ones we are given. Perhaps.

I climbed a set of designated stairs and took a seat sat on a closed-off balcony and waited.

The scene reminded me of every other human wedding I had attended: stiff, formal, uncomfortable shoes and frivolous hats. There was a small boy up front who kept unlacing his smock and throwing it off only to have mother tie it up all over again. I almost wanted to give him a smile, a real one that wouldn't haunt his dreams for life. But it was a fleeting thought.

The slow, respectable music began from the band, and I almost regretted attending. Queen Jinn arrived shortly and took a seat to my left and said nothing as the crowd settled down for the main event.

The Fairy Queen looked similarly bored and held her mouth in a taut, indifferent line. She was a tall creature with wavy, purple hair, yellow cat eyes, and dark skin that glowed iridescently. A bracken crown sat on her head, and two enormous moth wings sprouted from her back. She watched sullenly as the performance conducted itself onward.

Prince Jace arrived with his back straight and mouth an even straighter line. He looked like every other young man in his family line, and I didn't bother to memorize his face. He had licorice black locks and cool, blue eyes, an upright frame and straight nose. I didn't see anything like Tuck in his bearing, but I wasn't sure what I expected.

Jace took his place next to the minister and looked toward the end of the grand space.

The music erupted in a melodic silver jingle and I paused,

stilling myself for the next familiar clumsy footsteps. She was wearing heels this time, white and pristine and high as the heavens. Her gown trailed several people behind her, and she had flowers braided into her shimmering blond hair. Her dress was white, and the jewels around her throat were blood red, and they seemed to wear her more than she wore them.

"They plucked that one from the edge of the Thirteen Kingdoms," Jinn was murmuring, and we both exchanged a glance. "The Kingdom of Kiliok is not known for strength." Jinn smiled with all her teeth. "And the prince would bargain for beauty over the brawn of a nation, it seems."

I frowned slightly. Of course Jace's family would choose someone from a place like Kiliok. The country wouldn't be able to request much from them or use their queen as a bargaining tool. Kiliok was too distant and small—it would have very little voice at court.

Tuck walked steadily down the aisle, and I examined the pearls embroidered into the bodice of her dress and curve of the corset keeping her perfectly upright. She set a steady pace down the soft, white aisle, and I forgot to hold my expression firmly blank. She reached the altar just as the minister began his monologue outlying duty and country, heirs and gold.

"Are you going to curse them?" Jinn asked mildly as we watched on.

I shook my head. "They've paid their dues." I said without blinking. "I have nothing to gain from it." I looked at her. "You?"

Her spotted wings fluttered behind her. "I considered a blessing."

I glanced at her. "Oh?"

She glanced down. "Or a curse. I still haven't decided. I'll have to see my mood."

I gave a rumbling chuckle and turned away. "Do as you will."

". . . and do you Nadina Josephine Tulip . . ." I wondered which name truly belonged to her as the procession wound down to the actual kiss. It didn't really matter, of course; their lips met in the end and the crowd erupted into applause.

A new queen was welcomed into the family—however foreign she might be.

Tuck only paused once to look up and give me a very curious look as she passed, arm in arm with Prince Jace. I gave her a short nod and she smiled. I let it all pass and considered leaving then.

"Oh." I looked up as Jinn spoke mildly.

I blinked. "Yes?" I prompted her and watched her finely crafted features shift, her lips pulled down, and her pupils expanded. "Did you make up your mind?" I finally asked as she sat motionlessly beside me.

Jinn flashed a look at me and then turned her face away. "Humans make their own curses," she responded lowly.

My mouth twitched. "Ruins our business, doesn't it?"

She didn't laugh, and I didn't try to force it. Jinn smiled an alien smile and then left. The wedding of Nadina of Kiliok and Jace of Hessia passed without note for that night.

I watched the first dance and ate my fill of chicken and all the little lambs in the kingdom; I only stopped to tell one tale to the locals. It was a folk story of blood eating giants and the ghosts of lost maidens in my bog. The maidens in white turned out to be banshees at the end of course, and the look in the local's eyes when I got to that part always made it worth it.

Tuck didn't spare me another glance.

∞∞∞

I returned, exhausted, to my bog and waited for the next week. It came, and she did not. I waited for the next one, but no horse hooves or little, clumsy feet approached from outside.

I tried to let go of the strange Tuck girl and her brief fascination with oddities.

She was just another bored noble, after all.

The sun set and rose, and the days passed on. Days and days, and then winters that I stopped counting.

∞∞∞

I was older by then, still around four hundred, young for the ages and old for myself.

Her footsteps returned on the night of the rains, heavy this time and with a purpose to them. The vibrations across the wood were lumbering, the lightness of her step was replaced with a thumping sturdy gait. I lifted my eyebrows. It was different, but it was still her.

The water washed against the top of my bridge, and I curiously stuck my head out; raindrops pelted across my nose as someone stood directly above me. She hadn't bothered to stay in the neutral zone this time.

She bent over the railing, drooping like her limbs might fall apart at the seams at any moment, heavy, and fit together with bolts and screws instead of feathers. I looked up and thunder crashed in the distance.

I frowned. "This isn't really the time or place, little bird."

I tried to make her out and noticed the shape of her dress had changed— no, her body had changed. I tried to remember how many years it had been, but out of the dark night, I made out a distinct slope of her dress, outward, a belly extending down.

I drew myself up, "there is a storm. You should know—"

"Help me."

Her face was illuminated by a lightning strike, and her features came into sharp focus: swollen cheeks and hollow eyes, complexion pale as a blurry full moon. Her hair clung damply to her face, and some life had been drained out of her.

I should turn her away quickly, threaten her back into the castle. I ordered myself to dismiss her.

"Please," she said in a tiny voice threaded with pure exhaustion.

I pointed to the nearest bog tree instead. "Curl up there," I murmured. "Close your eyes."

I cast the protection spell around the tree before I even knew what I was doing. *I shouldn't,* I told myself, *I don't want to.* But the spot was soon dry and plush as the water veered away from it and a young woman curled up underneath the branches.

The hours slipped by as I watched Tuck fall into a deep troubled sleep under my watch. I didn't let the rain touch her.

∞ ∞ ∞

Many hours faded through until the morning sun eventually punctured the misty cloud cover and I turned back to the woman. Her eyes slowly opened as the light pierced through the tree branches and I stared discerningly down at her midriff.

"You're with child," I said dryly as I licked my lips, "the heir." I gestured downward and tried to put together my next question.

Tuck's eyes flickered back and forth in a type of panic and she slowly sat up. "It wasn't a dream." She clutched her loose shawl around herself.

"Shhh." I hovered closer. "You've simply had a bad night, little bird."

She glanced over at me and her eyes were as sunken as craters on the moon. "You," she said breathlessly, "Lamn."

I nodded slowly. "Among other names."

I watched carefully as Tuck's eyes filled with moisture and started to overflow, she curled up on herself and cradled her swollen belly. "I thought I dreamed you too."

I shook my head. "Tuck," I said calmly, and she looked up immediately, responding to what must have been an old name by then. "You carry the heir. Someone must be looking for you by now."

And I don't fancy being swamped by an angry mob right now.

She shivered from head to toe and I observed her thin wrists and puffy face. Something was wrong. She looked up at me with her bottom lip trembling. "It doesn't matter," she said in a hiccupping voice. "Let them look."

I frowned deeply. "What is it?" I asked, dragging my eyes over her sickly pale skin. "What is all this?"

She looked down at her lap, eyes burning, "Lamn, this child feels as if it might kill me." She said faintly, with a bow to her head. "It feels like it *is* killing me."

I waited for a moment, assessing her withered look, drooping posture, and the steel in her eyes. I took a deep, unhappy breath. "It is never easy."

She shook her head and the tears kept overflowing. "I can't sleep. The nausea is constant. He keeps moving. He's . . . it's not going right. It's all wrong."

I just pursed my lips. "I can see the sickness on you."

She let out a little sob. "Did you do this?" Her eyes crinkled, "I didn't think you cursed me, but . . ."

I just shook my head. "I am not the person you think I am."

She looked down at her lap again and blinked a couple times. "I know," she said and her voice cracked. "I told Jace it was me and not you. That I'm the reason for it." She hid her face in her hands, and I eased myself down next to her.

"Hush now." I patted her shoulder.

She painfully looked up with puffy, red eyes. "Please," she said in a voice I never heard her use before, "can you help me?"

I just nodded. I didn't want to. I knew I shouldn't. But it was too late—it had been too late for a while.

"Reed root," I said simply. "Mandrake placed in warm milk," I continued. "Honey mixed with temple rot, not the mold kind, the roots."

She wrinkled her brow. "The doctors have been working around the clock. Do you think . . . ? Do you know . . . ?" She grasped at something and searched my face.

I slowly raised my thin, gnarled hands up toward her. "And one last thing."

She blinked a couple times. "Yes?"

"My blessing." I whispered and sucked the light dry from the air around me. "Don't tell anyone."

The light hovered, brave and new, twinkling in the air around us like stars. I hadn't given one out in ages— not since I was fresh, and young. The light scattered in all directions and then sucked into her skin and pores as I said the words under my breath, welding them to her.

"Light, protection, breath," I murmured. "Light, protection, breath." I weaved her lifeline together so thick and golden that I thought she might live forever after that. I took a deep breath and opened my eyes that I hadn't realized I closed. "That child is not going to kill you, your majesty."

Tuck was still weeping. She was older somehow, so much older. "Thank you," she said breathlessly. "Gods, thank you."

I took her hand and repeated, "Mandrake soaked in warm milk, honey mixed with temple rot— just the roots." We shared a look that I couldn't describe, and I wanted to shatter that, too, gnash it up between my teeth and forget.

Her shoulders were thick and heavy looking, sloping down and finally releasing. "They wouldn't let me see you after we started trying for him. They said I had to stay inside the castle for the sake of my health." She held her belly again, and I just nodded.

"It's for the best." I responded tartly and looked away.

She sighed with the weight of ages on her. "I don't suppose Bog Hags have to give their lives for duty and country?"

I gave a sad smile. "Go back, little bird." I said and closed my eyes. "The grass is not greener in pastures you know not of."

She raised her eyebrows. "I always read Bog Witches were full of riddles. You've been holding out on me."

I gave a soft chuckle, and the old Tuck I remembered shone through this new, mature woman.

I reached, and I knew I shouldn't either, but it was too late now. I took both her soft, milky hands and I squeezed them, hard, not hard enough to hurt. But she needed to know.

"This child will not kill you," I whispered with a hiss. "You have my blessing. Use it."

She looked down toward her belly reverently. "Will he have it too?"

I frowned. "You shouldn't tell anyone."

She cooed softly. "You hear that little one?" She gave a smile that glowed at the edges. "You will be imbued with essence of Bog Witch."

I snorted. "You always were more daring than a box of feral cats."

She looked up, sadly this time. "Thank you." She said, face still swollen and eyes sunken, "I won't forget this."

I started to shoo her. "Go," I said quickly, something stirring within me, "before I change my mind."

She rolled her eyes but managed to lumber to her feet. "This won't be the last you see of me, Lamn," she said softly and began to walk. "Not this time." I watched her back as she retreated toward the bridge and towards her people.

My eyes creased and I exhaled. "It's Clemency," I called listlessly after her. "Lamn is the name of the bog."

She was gone already, and I had nothing but a sudden pain left in my chest. I closed my eyes and extended the blessing once more.

Tuck returned twice, once to tell me that the Mandrake screamed at her and to curse me for it, and another time to laugh so hard she almost fell into the swampy waters next to me. Jace apparently almost passed out when he saw her eating temple rot.

She got better.

I heard from afar that the next prince was born, just as the old King Gregory died. Tuck really was a queen now. It was a closed birth, a hard pregnancy and a hard birth. No one was invited to it.

I felt her distant footsteps now and then. Sometimes they came to the edge of the bog once more, but they never entered. I waited. I didn't dwell. I slept soundly as several winters passed in a blur.

I left once, into the city streets, disguised as a beggar woman, and I heard that the new prince was strong, rambunctious. He had his father's charcoal black hair and mother's smile. I tried not to catch his name, and I did anyway.

Clement.

I didn't dwell on it.

∞ ∞ ∞

I was steeped in the roots of a tree when I heard it again— something I thought had disappeared from my stratosphere forever.

"I can't," she spoke rapidly, breathlessly. "I tried to. But I can't, not again."

I turned around slowly, easily. I straightened up and oozed down the roots and back toward my bridge. I raised my eyebrows. "And here I thought you were a smart girl and were done with me."

Tuck's lips quivered. She was dressed in an olive-green gown and looked bright and full of life this time. "Never," she said softly, and I didn't know what to do with that.

"Huh." I grunted and turned away again.

She took a deep breath. "I tried to take him to meet you." She said steadily as she looked down from her perch on the bridge, "again and again. But they watch him more carefully than a hawk on a field mouse."

I sunk into the muddy waters. "As they should."

She frowned deeply. "They don't trust me."

I nodded. "A foreign queen stays foreign for a land like Hessia," I said grimly. "I know well of these people's superstitions."

She gave a tight smile down at the ground. "I started reading all those books you told me about," she said in a small voice. "They keep me sane."

"Did you ever figure out if Fairies are actually clever or not?"

Tuck looked up. "I did," she said slowly. "They are. But not as clever as they think."

I gave out a hearty laugh, a real one. "Smart girl."

Tuck tightened her hands around each other. "No," she looked away. "I was foolish."

I shrugged. "You were young," I said as I tilted my head. "Different, strange, and not sorry about it."

She grinned thinly. "Still am." She sighed. "But I made so many mistakes." She rubbed her knuckles together. "I never earned their trust."

I tilted my head to the side. "Why are you telling me this?" My jaw tightened.

"I don't know." She sighed heavily. "Perhaps I wanted one last confession, or maybe I thought it might change something. To go where it all began."

"What began?"

She looked up at the tree branches above. "It doesn't matter," she said bitterly and closed her eyes. "They want me to do it again."

I raised my eyebrows. "Do what?" I said flatly. "Wander into bogs again and bother ancient powerful beings?"

She laughed. "I wish!" She took a deep, heaving breath. "They need more than just Clement. Hessia demands multiple heirs."

"Oh." I nodded at that, affirming the truth I already knew. "Don't they know?" *Don't they know the first one was a hair away from killing you?*

She just frowned at her feet. "They don't listen."

I nodded again. "I can . . ." I hummed, "I can do it again." I should have added "for a price," but I didn't.

She tugged at a stray blond lock of hair. "I don't have it in me. Not a second time," she said, looking weary, eyes tired and hands falling still and open at her sides, "even with a powerful witch's blessing."

I put my hand out. "You don't know what I'm capable of." I flashed her an almost-smile. "You never did."

She hesitated, looking at my hand for a long second, and I should have pulled back, but I didn't. She took it. Our skin met and tingled like a wildfire, and it wasn't like the first time, like when I was trying to convey everything to her.

She held the dust and the grime and my long-gnarled fingers; she brought them up toward her face. "I've been reading," she said evenly, eyes unfocused. "Tell me then," she whispered into my knuckle, "how does a River Nymph descend into a bog?"

I didn't meet her eyes, but I tightened my grip. "With a bit of luck." I said warmly and she chuckled.

"Of course." She searched my face with her prickly, green eyes. "What kind of luck?"

I hummed deep in my chest. "It goes like all stories go. Life gives and takes. I lived peacefully for a time, but foolishly. There were men near the rivers who wanted with a want that carves out your flesh and digs out your soul. And then in turn I was given a blessing." I curled back my lips. "You already knew that secret though."

She nodded and her free hand raised up and grazed my cracked cheek. "I wanted it so badly." Her eyes shimmered and met mine, holding my gaze and passing something unnamable between us; I leaned forward, but didn't press any closer.

We held our breaths and waited for something that wasn't coming, wrapped in something we didn't understand. I clutched her hand so tightly I knew it hurt.

Tuck turned before I did, and we said a soundless goodbye. I threw my blessing at her one last time.

∞ ∞ ∞

Men . . . men are cruel. They fight and scream and ruin each other, arguing and crying to Gods, falling in love and then out, hurting, only to do it all over again. Men are cruel. So are the waves and the stinging snow and biting wind and unforgiving earth. The earth is also cruel.

Though men can be bargained with, reasoned with, the earth, on the other hand, will eat you whole without question. Perhaps that was what I liked about it.

Her footsteps came heavy this time, fast and pounding the water's bottom, shoes sucked into the mud and struggling with each step. She was breathing hard and dashing forward with lurching, hurried movements.

I woke with a start as dogs brayed in the distance. She hadn't been subtle, or perhaps the king had more eyes on her side than she knew. Either way, I could feel the thumping of men's feet in my realm and the calling of distant voices.

I surged upright and moved as fast as a roaring river.

"Tuck!" I called with the voice of thunder. "Tuck!"

I could sense someone else cradled in her arms and squirming. "Mama." I heard it now, clear as day. He was young and strong, as I knew he would be.

I used the trees as my eyes and looked toward the scene. I found them.

The eyes of the boy glowed yellow in the dark and Tuck sprinted across the swampy earth, away from the dogs and the harsh voices. I surged forward on a wave of water, approaching quickly just as the soldiers did. The mother and child were pinned between me and the king's men.

I gnashed my teeth as I met eyes with the distant footmen.

"I will grind your bones to dust and use your shins as my garden gate." I roared and the men faltered, but only for a moment.

"A witch!"

"I knew it! I knew the unnatural queen had allies on the Other Side."

I flared my nostrils and I lifted my hand, but so did the men. One young soldier raised a crossbow toward my chest and took aim right past Tuck's shoulder.

"Don't hit the child!" the captain cried as the young soldier was jostled from the side, and it all happened in slow motion.

"Clemency!" Tuck's voice rang out just as she reached for me, just as the arrow was let loose.

Her son's eyes went huge, shaking and frightened as the arrow pierced his mother's back like a sapling pierces the soft earth as it grows. A silent gasp spread across Tuck's face and then a shock of pain. Clement fell from her arms and she toppled forward. Red blossomed across the dark waters.

I gave out an unearthly cry, every inch of me tingling as I prepared to descend on the soldiers. I would make sure they were dead and eaten and discarded into the scraps of time and earth. I screamed and screamed, but I was not the only one listening.

Before my winds could wrench apart the woods, before the roaches could come crawling out of the trees and bog cats yowling out of the ground, before I could summon hell. The earth was listening, and the earth does not bargain, but it does give and take.

Much like a witch.

It encompassed her before I could even blink, the vines and leaves and waters swishing around her, covering her, folding around her from all sides.

I needed to rip out the throats of these men, but I picked up her wailing son instead. He was weeping and wiping at his brilliant yellow eyes and tearing at his dark hair, whimpering softly in an emotion I couldn't fathom from one so young.

"Shhh." I gathered him close to me. "It's beginning."

The leaves twisted, the waters rippled, and the forest became so deathly quiet I was afraid it might break. They call it the devil, but I have never seen the devil breathe life back into someone as quickly as he takes it.

Her skin fastened into thick bark; her hair twisted into streams of golden light, her face mixed into something otherworldly and unknowable, rough and hard in all directions. Tuck raised once more from the waters, and I was left breathless. She stood, bark and light and forest now, all forest.

She raised her head and smiled, smiled something brilliant and wicked. "I knew it," she said softly and looked down at her hands.

The soldiers scattered, running for their lives to tell the king of the betrayal; terror would follow horror. But that could wait. It all could wait. I shifted young Prince Clement in my arms and reached out on last time.

She took my hand. "Tell me," she said lightly, "can a Bog Witch fall in love? I read that they can't."

I smiled widely. "Let's find out."

We turned towards the deepest parts of the forest and

started walking, creeping into the unknown depths of a soft and distant world. The first kiss shifted everything inside me, and then the second one broke it.

Very few new footsteps arrived after that, for who would face the two most powerful Bog Witches in their home? Two witches and the next and future king.

About The Author

Jacquelynn Lyon

 Jacquelynn Lyon is an emerging author in fiction and poetry. She was born in Boulder Colorado and spent several years as a semi-feral child in the Rocky Mountains. She writes fantasy, science fiction, gay romance, and about anything that fills her with wonder. When not writing she spends her time jogging, reading, and watching her cat do a delightful number of cat-things.

Follow her on Twitter @JacquelynnLyon

Little Lights

Do not fall in love with girls on floating islands.
Do not grab her letter from the sky and chase her unknown out-line into the heavens.
Do not follow little lights into the darkness and lose your way—or find it.

Winifred Otiena lives in a city that shares a very special holiday with a floating continent: they send paper airplanes up to their sister land each year. The island in exchange passes down lanterns of every color back to earth. Winnie is young when she catches her first lantern and reads the note tucked away inside.

She is young when she starts to fantasize about meeting the girl who wrote it and eventually trying to reach her. As she grows older her search continues and her feelings begin to shift when her hopes seem fully realized. A story of a far-off future where two girls are separated by sky and land and how they slowly fall for one another—as well as rise.

9 798555 531124